Fanny, the Flying French Bulldog

by Nelson Bloncourt

illustrated by Nikita Polyansky

Glitterati

INCORPORATED

New York | London

First published in 2014 by

Glitterati
INCORPORATED

New York | London

New York Office:
322 West 57th Street #19T, New York, New York 10019
Telephone: 212 362 9119

London Office:
1 Rona Road, London NW3 2HY
Tel/Fax +44 (0) 207 267 9739

www.GlitteratiIncorporated.com
media@GlitteratiIncorporated.com for inquiries

First edition, 2014

Library of Congress Cataloging-in-Publication Data:
Bloncourt, Nelson, 1950-
Fanny the flying French bulldog / by Nelson Bloncourt ;
illustrated by Nikita Polyansky. -- 1st ed.
p. cm.
Summary: Fanny the French bulldog loves her new home
in San Francisco, but she misses her mother so much that
one day she embarks on an incredible journey.
ISBN 978-0-9851696-3-3 (hardcover)
1. French bulldog--Juvenile fiction. 2. Families--Juvenile fiction.
3. San Francisco (Calif.)--Juvenile fiction. [1. French bulldog--Fiction.
2. Dogs--Fiction. 3. Flight--Fiction. 4. Circus--Fiction. 5. Mother and child--
Fiction. 6. San Francisco (Calif.)--Fiction.] I. Polyansky, Nikita, ill. II. Title.
PZ7.B6224Fan 2013
[E]--dc23
2012034992

Hardcover edition ISBN 13: 978-0-9851696-3-3
Design: Sarah Morgan Karp/smk-design.com

Reprographics by Studio Fasoli, Italy
Printed and Bound by Gorenjski tisk, Slovenia

10 9 8 7 6 5 4 3 2 1

For Fanny, in gratitude for having been my most beloved companion, best friend, confidant, muse, and Buddha. We are forever together.

And to all the four-legged ones who teach us that life is in the moment. —N.B.

For my lovely daughter, Paulina, who loves this book so much. Thank you for all of your help. And to Preston Bailey for his support. Thank you to Leslie Budnick, our editor, for helping me to find my way home. —N.P.

Fanny is a French bulldog.

She loves to take naps in the sun, ride in her dad's convertible, and run on the beach.

Fanny lives with her dad in a cozy house on a hill in San Francisco.

He brought her home when she was just three months old. He said he chose her because he loved her big ears. Fanny loves her dad.

But sometimes, she wonders about the home she left behind and about her mother.

What would it be like to run with her in the grass
or play tug-of-war together?

Does she have big ears, too? Is she lonely?

One day in the garden, Fanny has an idea. If the butterflies and the birds can flap their wings to fly, maybe she could flap her ears to fly—maybe then she could find her mother.

Just the idea of seeing her mother makes her heart beat with so much energy that her enormous ears begin to flutter. She closes her eyes and thinks hard about her mom. She feels her body rise above the ground.

But not for long.

So she tries and tries and tries until . . .

...she flies!

Every time she wants to fly, she closes her eyes
and concentrates on her mother.

She flies over her dad's garden. She flies over Golden Gate Park. She flies over the Golden Gate Bridge.

She heads south over Lombard Street (the most crooked street in the country!), past Chinatown and Fisherman's Wharf, past the bay and the freeway, past the hillsides and the windmills.

As she soars she notices a curious,
striped building with little flags flying
off its peaked tops.

She hears music and laughter.

What is going on down there?

She peeks inside. She sees clowns, acrobats, and performers!
There are dogs, elephants, giraffes, and big cats with stripes,
spots, and manes—and they are all dressed in costumes!

It looks like so much fun.

A big lion approaches. "We are closed," he says.
"What do you want?"

"I saw your tent," says Fanny, "I want to be in the show."

He laughs. "Little dog, what can you do?"

"I can fly," says Fanny.

The lion snickers. "Don't be
silly. Dogs don't fly."

Fanny stands up, closes her eyes, flaps her
ears, and takes off. Flying circles over the lion,
she makes him so dizzy that he falls over.

"So what do you think of that?" asks Fanny.

"Little dog," the lion says, "I'm Leonardo the ringmaster and I will make you the star of the show. What's your name?"

"My name is Fanny." Then she adds proudly, "I'm a French bulldog."

He thinks for a moment and smiles. "We will call you Fanny, the Flying Frenchie!"

After practicing with the other performers,
Fanny is fit for her costume.

Then it is showtime.

"Ladies and gentlemen, children of all ages!" roars Leonardo. "Turn your eyes high above the center ring to.

Fanny,

Fanny, in her pink tutu, **soars** over the crowd to the delight and wonder of all that watch her.

The music plays. Fanny reaches for the trapeze bar with her shaking paws, takes a deep breath, grabs on tight and swings through the air! Back and forth. Back and forth. Back and forth.

Suddenly, she lets go.

The audience gasps.
Will she fall?

Fanny loves the music and the applause, but when she looks out at the crowd—at all the families—she knows that she has to be on her way. She wants to find her mother.

Fanny bids farewell to her new friends, leaving the music and the big top behind, smiling all the while.

She floats and flies until she spots
what she thinks is a familiar oak tree. I think this is it.

As she lands, she sees bunches of little puppies
frolicking together, while others snuggle up to their mommies.

Fanny walks towards one group.
Will I recognize her? Will she know it's me?

They clap and scream. And the more they applaud
the faster and higher Fanny flies.

Then, a few feet away, under the big oak tree, she sees her.

As Fanny comes closer, her mom stands still. When the two are nose to nose, her mom smells her. And in a moment of joy, she licks Fanny! They nip at each other's cheeks and roll around on the grass.

Lying close to her mom, Fanny tells her about her dad and all her toys and her favorite treats—carrot sticks—and how her dad rubs her belly until she falls asleep. She tells her about learning to fly and about the circus.

Tired from all of the excitement, Fanny snuggles into her mother and falls asleep.

When she wakes, her mother has a surprise for her. She takes Fanny to a spot where four little puppies play in the sun. She says, "Fanny, these are your brother and sisters."

Fanny can't believe it—sisters and a brother, too! She rolls over and the little ones jump all over her, covering Fanny with tons of little licks. They play until it starts getting dark.

Dad must be worried, Fanny thinks.
It's time for me to go.

Fanny and her momma give
each other one last lick.

This time, Fanny doesn't have to close her eyes and concentrate. She just looks at her mom, her heart fills with love, and off she flies ... past the tent and the windmills, over the water, toward her home and her dad.

Fanny is happy. She knows her mom is not alone, she knows she was star for a day ...

...and best of all, she knows she is loved.